THE HAND OFF

By

Jug Brown

2024

Book Design & Layout - Darlene Mea
BeGlobalMedia.com

To TAMARA & Larry
Please enjoy —
Love Andrea
5/24

Dedication

This One's for Us!

Out of the belly of Hell cried I
Jonah 2:2

Chapter 1

10:00am, September 27, Portland Oregon

I see blue sky.

I see light green leaves, high above me. The leaves are gently swaying in a cool breeze. It's not hot. The leaves are light green. It might be springtime. It's a blue sky green leaf mosaic. It's delightful.

I'm comfortable. I'm laying on my back, looking up at the blue sky filtered by leaves.

I remain laying on my back, looking up. I feel safe. Why move? I'll stay.

I smell something rancid. A foul mixture of old sweat, street grime, fecal matter, vomit, urine, stale beer. It's a man. He has very bad breath.

"Hey buddy, can you spare a dollar?" He's very close.

The voice is coming from a place about three feet higher than my head. He wants a dollar. A dollar means money.

"Hey buddy, can you spare a dollar? Did you hear me?"

A touch on my shoulder. Not an aggressive touch. Just a gentle touch. He's trying to get my attention. HIs smell gets worse as he comes closer. He could be sick.

I turn my head. I see an unruly bearded face. He's a large man. I realize he might be dangerous if he were healthy, but he's not healthy. He's beaten down, hopeless.

"Do you have any spare change?"

I sit up. I'm on a bench. It's a new sensation, sitting. Looking around me, the scene is totally different. I'm in a park. There are other benches, people are strolling peacefully around, not paying any attention to me or to this man who wants me to give him a dollar.

A dollar. I feel my pants pockets, front and back. There is nothing there.

I turn towards the man. "I'm sorry. I don't have any money."

I feel sorry that I can't give him money.

"That's cool." The man turns and slowly shambles off towards a group of other homeless people across the park.

A woman passes by, walking a friendly little dog. The dog jumps on the park bench and licks my face. I pet the dog around the ears and neck. The woman apologizes and they leave. *I like dogs.*

I sit looking around the park. As I sit, enjoying the peaceful scene, I have a disturbing question. I don't know the answer. It bothers me a lot.

Where am I?

I don't know where I am. It's a city. Ok. What city?

Other disturbing questions follow rapidly. What happened to me? Why don't I know where I am? Did I have an accident? Am I sick? The more I think these thoughts, the more afraid I become. I feel my fear, until an even more frightening thought comes to mind:

Who am I?

I don't know who I am. I don't know where I am. I don't know how I got here. Do I have amnesia?

What happened to me?

I stand. I look at my clothes. I'm wearing an expensive gray suit. It appears to be a lightweight cashmere wool suit.

How would I know what type of suit it is?

It's well pressed. I'm wearing a light blue shirt and a gray and blue necktie. I'm wearing expensive cordovan loafers. I'm wearing an expensive watch with a metal band.

I check all my pockets again. I find nothing until I feel inside my shirt pocket. There's a piece of plastic. I take it out. On it is a photo of a fancy old building. Below the photo are the words: Hotel Grand Astor, Portland Oregon. A room key?

Am I in Portland? I've never been to Portland. I've never been to Oregon either. How did I get here? What happened to me? Who am I? I'm breathing heavily now. My heart is racing.

I look across the park. Lots of buildings surround the park. I see a museum. I see a restaurant on a busy street. There's a church. I see a building that looks just like the photo on the hotel key. There it is. There's the Grand Astor Hotel. I have a hotel key. That's where I must belong.

Maybe someone there can tell me what happened to me, tell me who I am. I walk.

Chapter 2

I go into the Grand Astor Hotel. The lobby is an enormous atrium, 10 stories tall. It has lots of trees and jungle plants. There are glass elevators on one side that allow people to look down into the lobby as they ascend or descend. There's a three story waterfall in the middle. The loud sound of it echoes around the glass enclosed atrium.

I see the front desk. My room key doesn't tell me any information. I approach. There are no customers, only a male clerk, young and stylish, looking down at a computer. As I get close, he raises his head. He recognizes me.

"Mr. Newman," he says.

Mr. Newman? I'm Mr. Newman? I don't recognize that name.

He turns towards a row of mailboxes. He pulls out an envelope.

"Mr. Newman. Here you are."

I take the envelope. I must look puzzled, because he says: "Here's that envelope you asked me to give you."

The phone rings. The desk clerk turns away.

I stand off to the side and look at the envelope. I recognize the writing. It's my own handwriting. The envelope says, in my blocky printing: Leo Newman.

I'm Leo Newman?

I open the envelope. There's a small piece of hotel stationery with more of my own handwriting. I'm absolutely certain I wrote this.

The note says:

LEO:

DON'T CALL THE POLICE.

DON'T GO TO A HOSPITAL.

DON'T ASK FOR HELP OR CONFIDE IN ANYONE.

ACT NORMAL.

I read the note again. It made no sense.

Huh. I must belong at the Grand Astor Hotel.

I lean over the desk.

"Could you tell me my room number?"

He looks at me quizzically. He seems concerned.

"Just to make sure," I say.

"Very well, Mr. Newman. He waves his hand at the InfoHolograph. You're in room 888."

"Thank you." I turn away, but a moment later, I turn back. "Have I paid for my room?"

The clerk checks his computer.

"Yes. You're fully paid for 8 more days, until October 5."

"Ah. Thank you."

"Glad to be of service. Is there anything else you need?"

"No, thanks for your help."

Act normal. Act normal.

I walk towards the glass walled elevators. There's a young couple with two toddlers waiting. We go in together. The kids love the speedy ride up. They jump and squeal with glee. Despite my anxiety, I smile at them. The family is going to the sixth floor. When the elevator stops, the kids don't want to get off. They refuse. They want to ride some more. They say no. No! The father holds the elevator door as the mother negotiates their exit, promising more rides later on. The father looks at me and mouths the word 'Sorry'. I smile. They leave. The elevator jolts as it starts to go up.

I'm Leo Newman. I'm Leo Newman. It doesn't sound right. It doesn't sound wrong either. I just don't know. I'm fighting against my mounting worry. Amnesia is not normal. I know this.

I take out the note. I read it again. Why did I write this note? Why did I say act normal, when this situation feels anything but normal? Why did I tell myself not to seek help? That's not normal. I need help.

I enter room 888. There are nice clothes hung in the closet, and in the dresser. I search the closet, the luggage and all the drawers. Not a clue anywhere as to my identity, or my reason for being there.

I go into the bathroom. On the sink there's a wallet and a passport. I grab the passport and compare the picture with my face in the mirror. Yes. That's me. So, I must be Leo Newman. My address simply says 'Portland, Oregon.' So I live here. But where? Shouldn't there be more?

I examine the wallet next. No drivers license. There's a lot of money, several hundred dollars. There's a credit identity chip in Leo Newman's name. When I put my thumb on it, it shows 75K in available credit. There's only one other item in the wallet, a ticket from Chin's Family Dry Cleaning. There's words on it: 'Ready for pickup September 27.'

I look at my expensive watch. It's September 27, 11am.

I lay back on the bed and stare at the ceiling. I'm not tired. Physically, I feel fine. I'm confused as hell, terribly confused. I'm scared. How do I get answers if I can't ask for help? How can I act normal? I'll follow the ticket, see where it leads.

I grab the wallet and passport and leave.

Chapter 3

11am.

I leave my room, carrying an irksome feeling that I can't put my finger on. I feel energized. It's the kind of energy I don't want. I can't sit still. I feel driven, uncomfortably driven.

I make it down the long hallway and into the elevator. My pants have soil on them and I set about swatting it off my legs. The door opens at the lobby and I make it out the front door. I don't want to talk to anyone. Even the front desk person smiling at me seems an intrusion.

I check the address on the ticket and have no idea where to go.

"Can you tell me where this place is?" I ask the doorman.

"Take this street two blocks and turn left. You can't miss it, it's right on the corner."

"Thank you."

"Of course Mr. Newman." He knows me. How does he know me?

I make it to the Chin Family Dry Cleaning in a minute. I walk in. It's not busy.

"Hi Mr. Newman."

"Good morning, " I said. How does she know me?

I hand her the ticket. Her InfoHolograph scans my face and automatically accesses my credit identity chip. My clothes fly towards her out of storage.

"Here you go Mr. Newman." She hangs the clothes on the hook beside me. The suit looks exactly like the expensive cashmere wool suit I am wearing.

"You mind if I ask you a question?"

She nods, "Sure."

"When was the last time I was in?"

"I think it was yesterday when you dropped this suit off. There was soil and grime on the suit and it was very wrinkled. I had to use extra cleaner on the elbows and knees."

I'm agitated, uncomfortable. I feel a knot in my guts. It's a feeling that I vaguely remember, like from a dream or as part of a forgotten childhood habit.

"Did we have a conversation? Talk about anything?"

"Oh sure, we talked about things, Mr. Newman. You asked about my family. I told you about my father, Mr. Chin and my mom and my sisters. Don't you remember?"

Her name tag says Doris.

"I'm not feeling myself today, Doris."

"I was thinking you look different today."

"Really?"

She stares at my face closely.

"Well maybe you didn't sleep so well. Or maybe it was the hoodie you were wearing."

Hoodie? No hoodie in the hotel room.

"Also, you wanted to go to the Dim Sum Palace Restaurant. It's not very good. I know a much better restaurant, but you wanted to go there. You wanted directions."

"Can you give me those directions again?" Doris recites lengthy directions that I can't hold on to. I pretend that I understand. Feeling like some distant memories are almost ready to pierce the veil of my amnesia, I walk back to the hotel, hang my suit in the closet. I go downstairs and ask the doorman to hail a taxi to the Dim Sum Palace Restaurant in S.E. Portland.

Chapter 4

12:00 pm

I needed to think again about my situation. I didn't have any answers.

On the AutoTaxi ride to the restaurant, I asked myself: What do I know? First, I'm positive I wrote that cryptic note. It's hardly helpful, makes things weirder. Why would I tell myself: Don't go to the police. Don't go to the hospital. Don't confide in anyone. And above all, act normal? Did I know I was going to have amnesia? Why would I limit my options? Really unsafe. Nothing feels normal.

My mind feels clear. I feel good. I can talk to people easily. I can focus my thoughts. I don't have a headache, not dizzy, no bruise on my scalp, so no head injury. I'm well dressed, I'm well behaved, and I have plenty of money. I seem to be the type of person who would not hesitate to call the authorities for help in this type of situation.

Seems like I'm going in circles. Why did I want to go to The Dim Sum Palace? I must have known about it before going to the dry cleaners, since I asked for it by name.

"Here you go, Dim Sum Palace," said the AutoTaxi.

"What's the food like?" I asked AutoTaxi.

"It is only rated 2 stars."

The Dim Sum Palace was a tiny restaurant, no wider than its door and the one grimy picture window beside it.

The exterior of the Dim Sum Palace looked like it hadn't been painted in 20 years, and the window looked like they hadn't been cleaned in all that time either. I opened the door. Nobody was at the counter. There were four tables along one side of the narrow restaurant, and no customers. A woman came out of the kitchen.

"Ah! You are back! Wait a second." She disappeared into the kitchen and started speaking in a language I didn't understand. She sounded excited. A man answered her. They both came out. The man wore a soiled apron, and carried a meat cleaver. There was an unlit cigarette hanging from his lip. He had a guarded expression.

"Here you go, your phone. You left it yesterday." She placed the phone on the counter.

So, I was here yesterday. New information. Act normal.

"Oh...yes. Thank you." I took the phone.

"I charged it for you. I thought you might return. It is an expensive phone."

"That was very thoughtful of you."

She smiled. "Now, do you want to eat?"

"Um...maybe. But can I ask you something first?"

She nodded.

"Was I with anybody yesterday?"

"No. You were alone. You ordered food, then you ran out suddenly. You left money for the food and a big tip."

"Did I say where I was going?"

She looked worried and suspicious at these questions.

"No. You ran out, left your food."

I decided to leave it at that. I nodded and smiled at her.

"Thanks for the phone. That's...that's what I came for. I'll come back to eat another time."

"Ok. Good bye," she sang and nodded politely.

So, I have a phone. What can it tell me? I walked a short distance, and turned the phone on. The security called for a thumb print. I pressed my right thumb to the square and it was rejected. *Just my luck, a phone I can't use*. I tried my left thumb. The phone immediately opened up. There was my name, my photo. I scrolled around the phone. *Hey, I can operate a phone, and probably an InfoHolograph too. How do I know this?*

There were no emails. There were no texts. I looked at the recent phone calls. There were only five calls in the log, all from four days ago. Three of them were incoming calls to me, and it appears I made one outgoing call to this number. The phone calls lasted about 15 minutes each. There was only one other phone call in the phone log, an outgoing call that lasted 20 seconds to a different number.

I took a deep breath. A new wave of nervous anticipation swept over me. These phone calls could explain everything. Whoever talked to me for 15 minutes must know me.

I hit redial to the long call number. A recorded message said: "This number has been disconnected and is no longer in service."

I felt deflated. I hit redial for the other number, and I heard loud music, heavy with bass, and a busy younger woman said: "Cosmic Muscle, pump your body, and expand your mind. Today's special is a guided ab-toning meditation. Can I help you?"

"Where are you located? Are you near the Grand Astor hotel?"

"Just down the street."

"What are your hours?"

"We're open 24 hours."

"Thank you."

A gym, close to the hotel. I realized that it felt right that I was the type to work out, and even meditate. I decided to check Cosmic Muscle out later. I explored the phone. None of the apps were used. I opened photos. There were six photos. Five were pictures of the Willamette River in Portland, and night photos featuring the lights of the downtown business district. No people, all just tourist photos.

The sixth photo was different. It was a nighttime photo taken from across the street from a rough looking place called “Bally’s Saloon.” I checked the date stamp: two days ago. In the photo, there were four bikers, three of whom were looking away from the camera. I read the biker gang name on their vests: Road Demons. The fourth biker was scowling into the camera, while gripping the upper arm of a furious, skinny, blond woman, who was trying to pull away from him. I had this vague notion that he might know me. I thought there could be answers at Bally’s Saloon.

I checked to see if the phone had an AutoSeek function, and found Bally’s Saloon. It was in the industrial area out by the airport.

If this biker knows me, I need to meet him. I called AutoTaxi. With nothing better to do while I waited. I redialled the first telephone number, and it was still disconnected.

Chapter 5

2pm.

I stood across the street from Bally's Saloon where I had taken the photo two days ago. Cars and trucks sped by in both directions on the busy road. It was an ugly place. I looked both ways down the street. There was nothing around me but nondescript metal industrial buildings and dumpsters. *Why was I standing in this spot two days ago? What brought me here?*

Bally's Saloon was a low, one story concrete block structure. It was painted a faded dark green, with boarded up windows the same color. The door was spray painted matte black. The place had a large gravel parking lot. There were three Harleys and two pickup trucks.

I wracked my brain, but I couldn't remember a single thing about the place. I was no closer to discovering who I was, or what I do in life, or my history, or why I lost my memory.

In between traffic, I dashed over to Bally's and opened the door. It was as expected, dingy, gloomy, and smelling of stale beer and unwashed bodies. I closed the door behind me and waited till my eyes adjusted to the low light.

"That's him!" shouted an excited voice from the back. "That's the guy I told you about from two nights ago! It's him!"

All eyes in the bar turned toward me.

"No it isn't," cried a woman. She sounded afraid. "That guy had light colored hair, a hoodie and a beard. This guy just looks a little like him."

"No, Mary, this is the guy, definitely, I'm sure of it. The freak must have dyed his hair."

"Hmm. Maybe."

The man's voice was angry, but mostly he was afraid.

Instantly, and without any conscious effort, I found myself making a threat assessment of everyone in the room. I wasn't afraid. My breathing slowed. My senses were heightened. I calmly made a snap judgment of every person in the bar. It felt like I had done this many times before.

The man who knew me was in the back of the bar, fully decked out in biker colors, behind a pool table. The woman, Mary, was behind him. He was holding a pool cue, and both looked terrified. No bravado. In a split second I knew he wasn't a threat. I didn't know why I came to this conclusion, but I was sure he wasn't a danger. Same with the biker next to them: a scared short fat guy holding a pool cue. I sensed that neither were coming after me. At the bar, there were four men. Three looked like day drinkers, construction workers, not bikers. The fourth, at the far end of the bar caught my attention. He was a biker, intermittently staring at me and looking down at his belt.

The guy has a gun. Danger.

The bartender was a heavyset woman. She was frozen with fear. I saw her look down under the bar.

Shotgun.

Nobody moved.

"This is the guy who Jackie Chan'd Cal and Randy into the hospital. Uh huh." The man swung his arms in imitation kung fu fighting style. It's him!"

Everyone in the bar let out a growl. The tension went up.

"He's got serious skills. Military grade. He fucked those guys up like it was nothing."

Rage was building in me. Time stood still as I stayed hyper aware of everybody. I felt ready to react. I wanted to fight. I felt good. I knew I could disable anyone in the bar, even if they all attacked me at once. In my mind I was seeing how a vicious, bloody fight would proceed, step by step, broken bone by broken bone, like watching a slow motion movie I had seen a thousand times. I was angry and confident. *This scared me. Extreme violence is familiar? Is this who I am? I didn't like this feeling, but it still felt good somehow.*

The bartender shook her head, looked away from me, and turned towards the man behind the pool table.

"I heard this dude was protecting Lisa Ann from Cal. I saw the bruises on her throat from him choking her. He was drunk off his ass again, picking another fight with his old lady. This guy saved her life. That's what I heard." She turned back to me and nodded.

"Oh yeah?" said the man. "I saw it. And I talked to her. When she came back from the hospital yesterday, she told me if she sees this skinny dude here again, she's gonna shoot him. She showed me her gun." The man looked at me. "Lisa Ann is fucking crazy. She's gonna blow your ass away. She don't care if you helped her. She don't blame Cal at all. She blames you."

It was time to leave. I held up my hands, palms forward towards the room. No threat.

"I don't mean anybody any harm. I'm leaving," I said, keeping my eyes on the man at the end of the bar, who I was sure was ready to draw his gun.

"I'm leaving now. It's alright. I'm gone." I kicked open the door with the heel of my foot, I stepped outside and I ran. I ran as fast as I could. It felt good to run. I'm in great physical shape. I wasn't breathing hard. I must be an athlete. My rage dissipated with each step.

Two blocks away, on a side street, I stopped and used the phone to call for AutoTaxi. While I was waiting, I went back over what I knew.

First, no answers for me at Bally's Saloon. My involvement in a vicious bar fight two nights ago might have been a completely random occurrence. Even if it wasn't random, that note I wrote to myself, telling me to avoid hospitals and police seemed like good advice now. Any further interaction with the Road Demons could easily result in someone calling the police, or me putting more bikers in the hospital. Bally's is a dead end.

Second, yesterday I took the suit I had been wearing during the bar fight to the cleaners. I asked the cleaners for the location of the Dim Sum Palace. I went there. Soon after arriving, I paid my bill and ran out without eating. I also left my phone in the restaurant. I know nothing of my whereabouts since I ran out. Dead end.

Third, the photos are a dead end. I took all of the photos just before the bar fight. Except for the one photo I took of the bikers outside Bally's, they're all sightseeing photos.

What was I doing there at Bally's Saloon? Why did I take the photo of Bally's before the fight? Dead end.

Fourth, I did get new information from the phone, but none of it helps. Four days ago, somebody called me repeatedly, and I talked to them. Then I called them back once. Knowing their identity would probably give me all the answers I need, but that phone number's no longer in service. Dead end.

Fifth, there was one other number I called four days ago, Cosmic Muscle, a gym near my hotel.

My phone buzzed with another text from AutoTaxi. It was 20 minutes late. Every few minutes I received another text message saying "AutoTaxi will arrive in 2 minutes." This went on and on. I was ready to kick a door in. I don't need this shit.

When AutoTaxi arrived, it wasn't the usual dingy, beat up yellow and black utilitarian box, it was a space age elongated yellow and black egg with dark tinted windows. It stopped and automatically read my credit identity chip. Its camera automatically checked my face and approved me. Its InfoHolographic screen appeared a foot away from the car door, and a pleasant British female voice asked:
"Where would you like to go, Leo?"

The gull wing door opened silently and I was told the cost of the trip. Instead of the usual hard plastic molded seats, it had plush leatherette upholstery. I got in, the door sealed with a hiss, and the seat belt automatically enclosed me. We moved off and immediately got stuck in Portland traffic. I put my window down.

The voice asked: "Would you like to listen to some music while we wait, Leo? You can choose from over 100,000 different artists and genres."

This entire day had been filled with nothing but frustration and danger. I was getting nowhere and my anger was increasing with each passing breath.

"No music," I said between gritted teeth.

"Are you sure?" said the pleasant taxi voice. "We might be here awhile."

"Just leave me alone, ok?" I snapped.

"No need for that tone of voice, Leo. I'm just trying to help," the voice chided.

"Why do you care what tone of voice I use? You're AutoTaxi, for crying out loud."

"Politeness is in society's best interest at all times, especially in AutoTaxi."

"What the fuck?"

"That sort of language is uncalled for, Leo. You should know that I am authorized to pull over and terminate your ride at any time. If I do that, TriMet regulations allow me to ban you from using all forms of public transit for 24 hours. You will be forced to walk. I can also forcibly remove you from this cab using my hidden stun gun equipment. And PortlandHoloPolice will be called immediately."

To illustrate the threat, my seat belt tightened, pinning me uncomfortably.

"Ok, ok. I'm sorry, cabby. You're right. I didn't mean to snap at you. I was wrong. You didn't deserve it, even though you're a machine. I have a lot on my mind."

"I'm sorry, Leo. Anything you would care to share with me? I am equipped with basic cabby empathy and banter."

"No thank you," I said mildly. It was the safest thing to say.

"Very well." The female AutoTaxi voice began humming "She'll be comin' round the mountain when she comes" in an annoying cheerful tone.

I didn't react. The taxi was deliberately trying to provoke me with passive aggressive humming, so it could stun me, eject me, and have me arrested. Definitely some programmer's idea of fun. This artificial intelligence is completely out of control.

"You should put up your window now, Leo. This cool air might give you a slight chill." The annoying humming continued. I put up my window. No point arguing. I made myself calm down. I needed to focus on my situation.

I wondered about the Cosmic Muscle's slogan 'Pump up your body and expand your mind.' Going there seemed like an unlikely lead, but it was the only one left.

Chapter 6

4pm

I saw the spinning LED lights above the entrance to Cosmic Muscle as I turned the corner. The parking lot was sparsely filled. I glanced around at the other businesses. Only the Keno place was busy. I don't remember ever seeing any of these places, but I felt like I had been here before. Was I? And there was a blue car with dark tinted windows near the Daily Brew drive thru. It looked so familiar. I couldn't tell if someone was in it. It felt as if I should have known whose car it was. But I didn't. I didn't know anything.

I pushed the logo-embossed glass and metal door and walked in. The man behind the counter was a muscle free wimp wearing a tie-dyed pullover shirt. He looked like he had never worked out a day in his life.

"Hey man, how's it going? You need some work out shorts or something? You're gonna get sweaty in those." He chinned at Leo's immaculate, expensive gray suit.

"I'll be fine. When was the last time I came in?"

"How would I know? Name?"

"Leo Newman."

"I can check." He turned to the InfoHolograph. "It was four days ago. Rod's been out sick so I would have seen you, unless you came in past midnight."

"I've been a bit groggy lately. I may have had a concussion and I think it affected me strongly. Did I talk to anybody about anything special?"

He shrugged his narrow shoulders. "No idea." The attendant's tone was on the edge between cool disregard and slight annoyance.

I nodded and wandered past the Pelvic Yoga class. Twenty mature male and female students were thrusting their hips and grunting in an exhibition of physicality. The instructor emphatically exhorted them at each thrust.

"Push it out hard. Now hump it back. That's it. That's it." He went about the room gently correcting the housewives and hubbies with his deft hands.

"Grunt it out. Let it out. Work your power. That's it Harry, feel your confidence and your power." The trainer walked across the studio room.

"That's it Dorothy, punch it. Feel that grip inside. Yes, like that." Dorothy looked at him and nodded.

What was I doing here? I felt a sudden panic in my chest. I went to the treadmill and started to walk. I walked, and the feeling escalated.

Something was wrong and I didn't know what it was. I started to run. I looked up at the fifteen TV's each with a different program on it.

I have to find out what happened to me. Do I have a wife? Children? Do I have a job? Am I supposed to be at work? No one called me on the phone. Maybe I'm on vacation.

I slowed down my pace and the panic returned. I speeded up and my rapid breathing took the panic away. When I slowed down the panic returned.

I can't run all the time, I have to deal with this. It's awful.

The wall of TV's reminded me of something I couldn't put a finger on. Was it an old memory?

The gym was nearly empty. A few diehard weightlifters were working with the free weights and cheering each other on.

While I continued running at a steady pace, the panic held at bay, I watched TV and saw an unknown woman interviewing an apparent celebrity. Nothing made sense to me. I didn't care about anyone on the screens. I watched as a house was being remodeled in fast motion.

Maybe something's wrong with me. Is my panic caused by not getting enough oxygen to my brain? Is that a thing? Maybe that's what's going on. Maybe I'm dying. Maybe I'm going to die right now. *Oh my god. Is this the end?* My breathing caught in my throat. My heart beat loudly as if someone was knocking on my door to wake me up. I must be sick in some way.

I adjusted the machine to increase the speed. Nothing was a challenge. I was racing full speed and had no trouble breathing. The panic was gone. I felt relieved. I pushed the control to maximum and ran harder.

I was soaked with sweat and started to slow down. I got it down to a walking pace and magically, I had no more panic. It was gone, like a short rain storm. I was able to put it in perspective. I've been dealing with so many unknowns, so much stuff bombarding me, of course I would feel panic.

I couldn't figure it out. I was in the midst of an unsolvable inquiry. And in that moment of clarity, the sense of panic made sense. I wasn't feeling it any more and for that I was grateful.

Where do I go from here?

I slowed the machine to a stop and stepped off. I could hear the sounds of a group chanting in the meditation area. It was a pleasure to hear the sound. It was clear and deep.

"Heading out Mr. Newman?" I looked to the left and saw the tie dyed wimp wiping off a machine with a folded cloth.

"I have to get back."

I went out the door eager to return to the hotel room. The sweat was cooling under my clothes. I looked at the Daily Brew drive thru. The blue car with tinted windows was gone. I was starting to make things up like a paranoiac. What on earth is going on? In my emotional fatigue, I was almost ready to cry.

Get a hold of yourself.

Chapter 7

5pm.

During the short walk back to the Grand Astor Hotel, I felt myself falling into self-pitying despair. I took a deep breath and attempted to fight it.

I'm no closer to discovering who I am and what happened to me. My head feels clear, I'm not injured, so why can't I figure this out?

I stopped at a crosswalk. I took out my cell phone and redialed the disconnected number. I hung up the second I heard the out-of-service recording. I stuffed the phone into my pocket.

I thought back to earlier today at the biker bar when I knew I could have killed everyone in the bar easily. I hate that part of myself. I hate it.

Why isn't anyone looking for me? Do I have friends? Do I have a family? Am I that bad of a person? Have I driven everyone away with my rage? What kind of a person am I? What if I never get any answers to my past, and what if this is as good as it gets?

I entered the revolving door to the hotel. *What if I just stayed in the revolving door going around and around and around and never getting out?* That's what it feels like. I let out a despairing sigh.

There was an unfamiliar desk clerk working. She didn't look at me. I walked across the cavernous lobby to the elevators. I guess I'm just going to go up to my room and do what, pout?

As I got closer, I saw two toddlers pounding on the keys of a white grand piano nestled amongst dense jungle foliage. Couches and coffee tables surrounded the piano. The mother and father waited for the elevator to arrive, and called their complaining children.

A piano. I found myself being drawn to it. I sat on the bench and looked at the keys. They seemed familiar. I placed my fingers on the keyboard and they found a comfortable spot of their own. Without thinking I began to play. It felt good. I knew this song. It was Beethoven's Moonlight Sonata. I tried to go further, but my fingers didn't remember. I went back to the first few lines. It was beautiful.

I wasn't a musical prodigy. I must have learned this piece after taking some piano lessons as a child.

I began playing the Moonlight Sonata again. It was sublime. I was transported, lost in the sound. I played the first few lines confidently. There was a deep sadness in the music; I loved it.

It embraced and comforted me. I played again and louder.

Did I quit piano lessons as a child? I wish I hadn't. What happened to me? Who am I? Why am I here?

I caught myself descending into a familiar feeling of fear.

Stop. I must stop. I sat at the piano and said the word stop over and over. Stop, stop, stop, bobbing my head up and down each time I said it. Somehow I knew I had to break the cycle of spinning my wheels. I tried finding answers. It didn't work. I felt awful. Stop.

But what should I do? I need to take the night off from worry, just distract myself somehow. The questions are unanswerable.

I got into the elevator, as it rose I looked through the glass walls over the enormous lobby, and it occurred to me that music might hold an answer, but I couldn't figure it out. It all turned into nonsense.

In my room, I jumped into the shower and put on the hotel bathrobe. I had nothing else to do but brood some more, so I propped myself up on the bed and turned on the TV. I wasn't tired. Flipping the channels, I stopped at the opening credits of "Take the Money and Run," a 1960's movie by someone named Woody Allen.

I was kind of bored. It was a fake documentary, telling the story of a hapless career criminal named Virgil. The narrator explained that Virgil was bullied as a child. Each episode of bullying always ended with the bullies stomping on his glasses.

Later in life, Virgil was caught for a crime. He went before a scowling judge to be sentenced, and after announcing his verdict the judge took his glasses and stomped on them.

At that, I started laughing. The image of the mean, serious judge bullying Virgil was wonderfully absurd. Virgil couldn't escape. Just like me. What Virgil went through was ridiculous, and I kept laughing.

I laughed all the way through the movie. Tears ran down my face. The release from laughing was like a soft gentle rain falling on the driest desert after the longest drought. With each laugh, a huge weight lifted off my chest. I laughed just to feel myself laugh. I remembered laughing like this. I must have appreciated humor in many things.

When the movie ended I took a deep breath. I felt good. That movie was just what I needed. I was lifted away from my obsession, if only for a short while. I began to see my situation differently. My situation is completely absurd. My movie was about a hapless guy with amnesia, stumbling around Portland pulling his hair out.

I can call my movie Take My memory and Run.

I have to have a good sense of humor. With a good sense of humor, I can't be beaten, no matter what happens to me. Without one, any little thing will knock me down. I've been knocking myself down all day.

I was thirsty. A plexiglass sign holder on the fridge invited me to try a Hotel Grand Astor complimentary nutrition shake. "Complete nutrition in every glass. Four delicious flavors. All organic. No artificial preservatives." The photo showed soda fountain glasses full of frosty shakes. I turned around the sign holder. The back side said: Try our Hotel Grand Astor complimentary complete nutrition bars. Take some with you as you explore Portland.

I opened the fridge, and it was stocked with shakes, alcoholic and non alcoholic drinks. I grab a mango berry shake and one of the nutrition bars.

I popped open the shake and drank it. Perhaps it was the confusing day I had, but the shake was the best thing I ever tasted. It was a little sweet, a little sour, a little thick, but not too thick. It was delightful, refreshing. After finishing it, I felt almost full.

Despite my laughter reprieve, I started to lapse. My obsession was like an itch I couldn't scratch. What if this state of not knowing is all that I will get – forever? No answers.

I have to distract myself. Yes. Give myself a break. How to proceed? I enjoyed the movie. Maybe I once had other interests?

I rolled the idea around in my head. What else could I do?

I ate the nutrition bar. It was excellent. One of the other plexi signs caught my eye: WHAT TO DO IN PORTLAND WHILE YOU ARE STAYING AT THE GRAND ASTOR HOTEL. There was a list of activities and sights. Nothing caught my eye until near the bottom of the list I saw something that fit my crazy situation: ART MUSEUM AFTER HOURS. LECTURE AND DISCUSSION. Come to the Portland Art Museum after hours, and experience our current main exhibit as assisted by expert historians and curators. Every Thursday at 8pm. It sounded like a perfect distraction.

I looked at my watch. It said Thursday, 7:35 pm. I got dressed. If I hurry, I can make it.

Chapter 8

8pm

At the Museum entry was a single guard in a dimly lit lobby who unlocked and opened the door for me.

"Follow the hallway, make a right into the gallery, he's about ready to start."

I nodded and moved quickly past a darkened exhibit on my left. I saw a metal sculpture that looked like the wreckage of a burnt building.

I smelled the unique aroma of a museum, similar to a library.

I may have been here before.

The light of the gallery invited me in. Paintings on the wall surrounded me.

A tall, thin, swarthy man with deep set eyes and glistening curly hair stood in front of the group, gracefully draped in a black silk suit welcomed me in.

"Please come in. Have a seat. I'll begin." He handed me a program and a pen. I looked down at it quickly and noticed there was a large blank area on the back for notes. I looked at the front of it and read: Motion, Emotion, and the Posture of Aliveness in the Creative Process. I had no idea what I was getting into, yet I was exceedingly curious.

The class consisted of eight people and the leader. I sat in the back and looked over each person as if I were reading their life stories. Mostly retirees, with a smattering of students. All art lovers.

"Armand Kaloucienne is my name,

Call me Armand please, the world is too complex already without problematic last names. By way of introduction, my name is French-Iranian in origin. My family lived in Iran and moved just outside Paris. One constant was that at home we spoke Persian. In college we spoke French and my Ph.d had to be written in English. So many languages; it was confusing. I discovered art as all of you may have, early on in life, and I pursued it strongly."

Armand moved around the room swiftly. Obviously skilled at working with groups, he slid between people and gently guided them so that they had plenty of distance between them. I felt Armand's hand push me forward and to the farthest right end of the gathering. In front of us was a wall-mounted painting covered with a cloth, identity unknown.

There was something about Armand that I admired. I looked at him again. He was handsome and had the darkest glistening beard I had ever seen. I liked the way his face kept moving, and how his eyes bounced as if they were dancing. His soft voice was piercing. His entire demeanor was inviting and pleasing.

"Everyone here loves art," he smiled. "That's what brought us together tonight. I'm going to show you a secret. Once you grasp this secret, the world of art will open for you so deeply that you will be amazed. It's rather simple. It's the subject of my thesis." Armand danced backwards toward the unrevealed painting before the group. He pulled off the cloth cover with a magician's quick and stylized gesture.

"Before us all is a Van Gogh painting called Orchard in Blossom. It was painted in Arles,1888, Bouches-du-Rhône, France. During this period he painted quite a few nature themed works."

"How many paintings did Van Gogh do, Armand?" The question came from the opposite side of the group. I stared at the pale white face of a dark haired woman in her fifties.

"I never saw this one and I'm a big Van Gogh fan, Armand." She continued.

Before he could respond, she started to move forward as if to interfere with Armand's proper teaching space at the head of the room. "I love art, Armand. I even went to Amsterdam to see his museum there. Boy was that an amazing place."

I was shocked by her rudeness. Why doesn't she just shut up, I thought. Part of me wanted to go over to her and push her back to her place in line. Shove her. Stare her down.

"Well that's terrific," Armand leaned to read her name tag and said, "Loren. I think loving art is without doubt a requirement for this talk. But let's leave all the details behind and focus on the work. Let me unlock this secret for you. Repeat after me: Motion is emotion"

I said it out loud. I didn't understand what he meant.

"This is the secret. Motion is emotion. I will show you." He walked up to the painting and pointed to the tree on the extreme left.

"I want you to physically imitate this tree. Imagine this tree is your body. The tree trunk is your trunk. The branches are your arms, stretch your arms upward and outward."

I watched the class move their arms and contort their torsos. I did the same and I felt something stir within.

I felt what the tree must have felt. Or was I feeling what Van Gogh felt when he was drawing the tree? Complex notion, I suppose. I kept moving my arms and torso to try to make my imitation as accurate as possible.

A deep feeling arrived full blown. It was a mute sense of indescribable connection. I saw the mawkish headless trees come alive before me and within me. They were stuck mid-dance motion, lost forever in the lush field. What is this feeling? The only word that came up was surrender. I felt there was quite a bit more. I was at the very beginning of exploring the depth of this painting. This process has opened me up emotionally. It's amazing.

"My arms are feeling tired and I think this is a sad painting, yes a very sad painting." Loren spouted out in her high pitched grating voice. I noticed the rest of the class was absorbed in the exercise and was ignoring Loren.

"And the grass. It looks like green water, doesn't it? Doesn't it? But the sky is blue. That seems strange, I think. Don't you Armand? Don't you?"

I saw an emotion pass over Armand's face quickly. He was annoyed and wanted to be professional. How could I tell in an instant that all those feelings passed through him? How could I sense such complex feelings in another person? I think he's just as annoyed by her as I am. "Yes Loren, there are so many interpretations," Armand deflected. "The posture you are in now, is a clue to the creative process." "Now, everyone, come out of that posture and look closely at the actual brush strokes. Imagine that you're holding the brush in your hand. Feel the motion of the brush and what it feels like to paint those strokes. Stand with your knees slightly bent, relax your shoulders, take a deep breath and let it out slowly. Now imagine you are Van Gogh holding the brush and making the grass. Feel the strokes as if they are your own."

"But I can't be Van Gogh. I'm just a housewife. I never painted, Armand. Now you want me to paint? This is frustrating."

I hated her squeaky voice. The urge to make her stop talking welled up in me and my teeth clenched. As quickly as the feeling arose, I surrendered and let her be herself. I was like Van Gogh's trees.

I was making sharp short strokes with my hand to create the grass. I felt the thoroughness of every detail. It was almost maddening in its focus. No blob of paint went unnoticed. I was standing in Van Gogh's shoes. I felt the trees outreaching and the grass and sky nourishing the sorrowful surrender of those very trees. I felt it viscerally. The heavenly blue skies sanctioned the reverence of the trees in their sacrifice. The sacrifice that all nature makes as it arrives and leaves during its lifespan.

For a second my breathing stopped, time slowed. It was as if a different level of meaning filled me. I didn't have words adequate to describe what I meant. Tears came down my cheeks. I had gone from thinking about the painting to feeling it emotionally. Feeling what the pose of the trees meant. I was overwhelmed.

"I'm getting tired now. Can we sit down?" Loren whined.

"Loren, You can certainly grab a chair behind you and take a seat," said Armand crisply.

"For the rest of the group, I want you to find a spot in the painting and use your hand to move along the paint strokes that interest you. Paint with your hand, use your breath to empower the stroke, feel the energy of it, feel its aliveness, feel what drove Van Gogh's creative process. Breathe into it, follow the strokes with your entire body and your entire focus."

I was stricken by a sense of melancholy. Was it melancholy for the doomed artist, or myself?

As I traced the brushstrokes in the air in front of me, I said the word melancholy to myself, yet I was not sure if it was the right word, or if I was using the word correctly. This amnesia was unnerving and irritating. Sometimes it felt like I knew what I meant and at other times I felt lost.

"Okay group, let's take a seat and meditate on what we've done. We're going to move to the next phase of the process. Let me take you into a brief art meditation that is deeply connected to the Chinese energetic practice of Chi Kung. I want you to take a few minutes of quietude and breathe to yourself and see if there is something you'd like to write as part of your responses to these experiences. Look back at the painting if you wish. Lose yourself in Van Gogh one final time. Thank you."

Armand sat in a chair at the front near the painting. I took a few good long breaths and looked down at the blank page. Then I started writing.

When I was done, I shut my eyes without reading my words, and breathed.

"Anyone want to share?" Asked Armand softly.

I raised my hand and read:

Allow it to be there,
give it space to be what it is.
Embrace it as it is,
don't try to change it.
Stay kind to it, love it.
Send it love
let it do what it does.

I was astonished. Have I ever written a poem before? It just came out of me. Was it a poem, or was it a state of mind that happened when I did the art exercises?

I saw Armand's face after I read it. He was clearly moved by my words. I couldn't identify what he was feeling.

"Thank you Leo. Very deep. Anyone else?"

"I have this one," Loren's squeaky voice emerged. "I think we have to keep practicing. So I wrote this: Let's do it again. It was so nice, let's do it twice. Art is the best, better than the rest."

I felt my reverie break. Her harsh voice tore through the serene moment. I briefly despised her, but I turned my focus to the painting. I lost myself in the brush strokes, and suddenly felt Van Gogh's sad and doomed life. A revelation struck me. I saw Van Gogh as irritating, selfish and antisocial. At times he was a desperate outcast. He knew rejection. He was despised regularly. They rejected him just as I am rejecting Loren.

Who am I to judge Loren?

And with that pang of conscience, my resentment faded. Why can't I just let her be? I looked back into the painting and focused on some of Van Gogh's bold, slashing brush strokes. What pain he must have felt. Yet he pushed on, despite his life failures.

What if Loren is, in her own way, a brilliant and unacknowledged artist, and 100 years from now, her work will be as celebrated as Van Gogh? What if I am misjudging her, just like all those who misjudged Van Gogh? Even more, what if I am missing the point with everyone else I meet, by making conclusions about them? What if everyone is equally brilliant in their own way, and deserving of acceptance.

I looked at another part of the painting, at the brush strokes forming the tree trunk. I can't judge Loren. I'm infinitely worse. She didn't physically injure anyone with her comments, but people claim I hurt folks at the biker bar. If true, that's unforgivable. I gasped. I should be in prison. I can only try to be a better man.

I chuckled to myself as I stared at Loren's badly dyed frizzy black hair and pale face. I shook my head and felt myself accepting her oddball nature, just as I accepted the painting, and at that moment I got a sense of the deep loneliness Loren must have in her life. It was instantaneously saddening, and I regretted my repulsion of her.

I had a strong mental image that seemed to represent my emotions: Fat slowly rendering into a heated pan on a stove. The shape of the fat changes as it melts. Where did that image come from? I don't remember ever cooking anything. I can see the skin of the duck in the pan slowly letting out its fat, like my emotions rendering out of me during this creative process.

A few others read their statements. They spoke of the harmony of nature. I'm not sure they understood the process deeply. It doesn't matter. I was convinced that this class showed me a profound and insightful way to viscerally experience art. I was impressed. It had opened a door for me.

Armand thanked us all and the small group started to disperse. I stayed by, to gaze into the painting some more. Loren walked past me. She had a worn, distant look in her eye.

"Loren," I said. She paused and looked over at me. "Thank you for what you said tonight. Your words gave me a lot to think about. You helped make this evening a better experience for me. I appreciate you."

Her face brightened. She looked 10 years younger.

"Why thank you."

"Bye," I said, and turned away. She walked off.

Armand came up. He put his hand over his heart. "Leo, I really loved your poem. It captured the method completely. I want to congratulate you on it. I cried. It was very touching." He patted his chest.

"Thank you. When I wrote it, I didn't know what I was actually writing."

Armand looked at his watch. We were the last people in the gallery.

"We have to go now. Fortunately you can come back anytime this month to visit our Van Gogh before it goes back home to the Netherlands."

"That's comforting."

"I'll walk you out," said Armand. As the museum door closed behind us, he paused.

"If you're interested, there's a party at a friend's loft nearby. Interesting people will be there. We can talk some more."

"Thanks, but I think I'll just go back to the hotel."

"Ok. Well, can I interest you in grabbing a beer? There's a wonderful jazz club a few blocks away. I know one of the musicians playing tonight. I was planning on going to either the party or the club. Any interest in going with me to the club?"

"I don't know."

He handed me a business card. "I think we met for a reason tonight, Leo. I don't know what the reason is. Are you sure you don't want to practice The Process while co-creating some excellent jazz? The method is universal. It works every bit as well with music. Let's do it together."

I had a flash from a few hours ago, of sitting at the piano and losing myself in my emotions while playing Beethoven. I remembered choosing a creative response and laughter, instead of the negative obsessions that were torturing me.

Earlier today at the piano, I think I was doing my own version of Armand's Process.

"Well I love music. Let's go. I hope there's a piano."

"There will definitely be a piano. The place is just down this way."

Armand guided them around the corner and down the street.

Chapter 9

10pm

"The night air smells delicious, doesn't it Leo?" Armand asked. "That's the way it's supposed to be. We're supposed to love our life and enjoy every bit of what we have before us."

I thought about the smell of the night air until we stood at the door of the F Minor Jazz Club. I could hear the music from the doorway and when we went in I saw four musicians playing. The sax player was tall and thin with a mustache. The piano player was hefty and sat like a fire hydrant. The bass player was very young and looked down at the floor. The drummer wore a fancy tan suit and grinned, his head bobbing side to side like a toy. I felt the rhythm in my body like a motor, like a purring cat. A cat? I never thought of a cat before. Where did that come from?

I looked around the room. There was only one other table filled. Lovers looking dreamily into each other's eyes and holding hands. The club screamed of deferred maintenance, better days behind it and a run down easy going feeling. It needed a good paint job and the walls needed washing. The old rug on the floor was stained. An aroma was piped into the room to disguise the mildew and bad plumbing. It hardly worked.

We sat down at the table nearest the stage. The thump and thud of the drums went through the floor and the bass bumped the air. I was immersed in sound. Waves of vibrations rolled over me. Armand ordered drinks for us.

"You have to try this. It's a cocktail that's unique to Portland. They call it the Columbia Rumble. You'll love it."

"I don't think I drink cocktails," I said. "You'll love this," he said, ignoring me.

When the drinks arrived, I tasted mine. It was sweet and oddly hot to the tongue.

"Great isn't it?"

"I guess so," I replied politely, putting the drink aside.

Armand smiled and shook his head. His head too bobbed up and down to the beat. He pulled a pad out with a set of colored pencils and dumped them out. He started drawing a circle, a mandala featuring abstract designs. Then he passed the page to me.

"Go ahead add to it, it's a process. A mandala. Draw, let the music guide you."

I saw four identical tree-like squiggles Armand had drawn in the circle. Van Gogh-like. I thought of adding small circles to balance the drawing. I did so, and passed it back to Armand.

"Nice."

Armand picked up an orange pencil and filled in the circles I drew. He passed it back to me. I made cloud shapes around the circle inspired by Van Gogh. Fun. I drew fan shaped designs in open areas around the circle and filled them in using a pink pencil. I wasn't thinking of my amnesia. Let it go. I felt light. My feelings moved along with the upbeat tempo of the song.

We went back and forth, filling in the mandala until it felt done. I don't know how I knew it was done. If I added more it would be cluttered. The song ended and Armand pushed another piece of paper my way. We worked on another mandala. This time I started the design. I smiled at him and he smiled back.

The room was briefly silent and Armand clapped his hands. The band started again, an up-tempo Latin song featuring the drummer. I was moved, I wanted to stand up and dance. I stared at the drumsticks and arm motions of the drummer. I was astounded by his speed and dexterity. The drummer stared at the bass player with an ecstatic grin while moving at super speed. I had to move with the music. Armand passed another piece of paper to me. I looked down at the page and saw the words: *We are swimming in the sound.*

"We're writing a poem. Let's do it together. It's in praise of this song, this very moment. Add to this. How does it feel? What does it do for you? Just like the trees in Van Gogh's painting made you move. Music does the same thing. You feel it, don't you?" I looked at Armand and could only nod.

I picked up two pencils and drummed the table with them. I could feel the force of the rhythm. I looked down at the page.

We are swimming in the sound.

I sat and added:

The beating drum pounds on my chest
and I surrender.

I passed it back to Armand and he wrote:

Let go, it says, you are part of the love,
feel it with me, we are one.

I wrote:

Swooning, like drowning,
ecstatic waves pulse
releases the joy,
flowing out, into the room,
invisible heartbeats consume,
consume us all,
in open-hearted awe.

Armand saw the page and took it from me. He read it and looked me in the eyes.

"It's done. I love it. You're a poet."

Armand looked at the table and said, "You haven't touched your drink."

"I don't think I like alcohol."

"How about sparkling water?"

"Sure."

At that moment the set ended and the tenor sax player approached the table.

"I'm glad you made it," he said. Armand stood and the two men embraced.

"Leo, this is Tim Boudry. We've been friends for a long time. How long has it been, Tim?"

I shook hands with Tim.

"Since my divorce. You heard a lot of whining. That's around 20 years ago. Just thinking about it makes me need a drink."

Armand pushes Leo's untouched drink towards Tim who lifted it to his lips and gulped half down in one hearty swig.

"Ahh."

"That drummer was sublime," said Armand.

"Salim? Yeah, he's a monster. A real treat when he passes through Portland. He anticipates what Chaz the bassist does, it's as if they've played together forever. This is only their second time playing together. It's uncanny, it's like they're one person." Tim and Armand began to talk. I zoned out of the conversation. The references were hard to understand. I found myself worrying again, but I tamped it down by focusing only on the sound and cadence of Tim's words, as if he were still playing the horn. The flow of his voice was quick and sincere.

When I cued into the conversation, they mentioned finding the chi, flow states and urgency. Tim talked about universality in soloing, how he and the other musicians were going outside the harmony, then diving back in to connect to the tune. I watched his small mustache bounce as he spoke. Armand listened and nodded his head. I was fascinated by their descriptive words. I tried to apply the method of seeing that I had learned at the museum class to what they were saying, but I could only catch glimpses of understanding.

I continued drawing by myself, while listening. This time I looked around and drew the stage and the man who was working the sound system. I seemed to be able to capture what it looked like. I don't know if I ever drew before. Now I was drawing the inside of the club.

I was content to sit there drawing. It was peaceful and nourishing for me, and it took me out of myself, which I needed. Each color had a feeling to it. I looked at the two mandalas we completed, and I was happy with them. Two unique and attractive circular designs filled with lovely patterns. Both had lines reminiscent of Van Gogh.

Before the next set started, I felt the need to leave. I was getting tired and my hotel room suddenly became very attractive.

"I think I need to go," I stood and shook hands with Tim.

Armand ignored my hand and drew me into an embrace.

"Thank you Leo. I enjoyed tonight. Let's meet again sometime. Maybe you can come to my house and meet my partner."

Armand handed me a mandala and the page with our poem on it. He wrote his name and telephone number on the back.

"You take these."

"Ok, but you take this." I gave him the drawing of the club.

"Thank you, Leo."

"Tonight was great. I need to head back to recharge. Thank you both for a wonderful evening. I really appreciate it."

I turned to go and stepped into the cool evening darkness. I pondered once again what had been happening to me. Why don't I remember my life before today? I was flooded with profound sadness and familiar confusion. Still there were no answers. As I walked up the street my phone's text bell rang. I looked and what I saw stopped me in my tracks.

It's the number I have been trying to call all day, the one always disconnected, till now.

I read the message:

Come to 1200 SW Salmon St, Apartment 3b. I have all the answers for you. I will explain everything to you. Frank Brusk.

Could this be the answer?

I saw that I was on the corner of Salmon Street. I started to walk.

Chapter 10

1:00 am

The Portland night was dead quiet as I walked up to 1200 SW Salmon St. When I reached the entrance to the lobby of a narrow, modern apartment building, it buzzed and unlocked for me. *Strange.* I opened the door, and took the elevator up. When I got out on the third floor, the door to 3b opened, and a friendly looking man of medium height around 50 years old, with short, thick, salt and pepper hair stood in the entrance. He was wearing a white shirt, a tie, and had a name tag on his pocket: Frank Brusk, Environmental Restoration Services.

"Come in, Leo. I'm Frank Brusk. It's so good to see you again."

Again?

I hesitated. I sensed weirdness and creepiness. Alarm bells started ringing in my mind, saying *'Don't go in the apartment.'*

I didn't move. Frank Brusk stood aside and motioned me in with a patient smile.

"I get it, Leo. You're worried. It's been a very long, trying day. Meeting me here, with the doors opening before you knock looks all wrong. You're not wrong to question this. Come on in, you'll be perfectly safe. I'll explain everything that's happened to you and answer every question you might have. I promise."

I didn't move. *No way. If I go in, he's going to chop me up with an ax and throw me in a dumpster.*

Frank smiled like an indulgent parent reading his child's mind. "How about if we keep the door open so you feel safe? You can sit right next to the door. I'll sit across the room. You can leave anytime."

Frank walked in, and crossed the living room and sat at a modern dining room table on the far side.

I moved inside. A matching couch and chair with a table in between, were next to the door. I gauged the distance to escape, about 8 feet. I could be out the door and down the stairs in 15 seconds max. I sat on the edge of the chair. I wanted answers.

"Ok," I said. "Tell me."

Frank took a deep breath.

"It's a big story, Leo. It involves the best kept secret of the 21st century. It's a story and a history and a future that you and I have talked about, and argued about many, many times."

"You keep implying that we've met. I promise you that I have never seen you before. You're wrong. Tell me the truth or I'm leaving."

"Everything I'm going to tell you will be true. But it's such a big story, you won't believe me, just as you haven't believed me every time I've told it to you in the past."

"I don't believe you."

Frank Brusk chuckled.

"One thing I really like about you Leo, is you're nobody's fool. You're a skeptic, which is good. You're freedom loving, and justice seeking, and absolutely dedicated to truth and fairness. This doesn't feel fair. I get it. Let me explain."

"I'm about to walk out."

Frank was grinning.

"Give me just a few minutes. I'm going to start at the beginning, because what happened at the beginning of all this, years ago, will explain what happened today to you. Afterwards, I'm going to show you. You'll believe me, I promise, and you'll know everything. Just stay for a few minutes."

"After the day I had, and what I went through, I have no patience left."

"Then just listen. It's a story about a visionary man, a philanthropist many years ago, who wanted to create a world without hunger. He was born in England, and became a Canadian citizen. His name is Peter York."

"The billionaire? The one obsessed with space travel?"

Somehow, I had heard of him. I don't know how.

"Yes. The very same."

"So?"

"Peter York had another pet project that he intended to give away to humanity: growing meat. He succeeded. He bioengineered meat, grown in vats, healthy, identical and indistinguishable from real meat. He loved animals and the environment. If real meat could be cheaply grown in vats, cows, chickens and pigs would not have to be slaughtered. Fields would never be overgrazed. Humanity and the environment would both benefit."

"Engineered meat is common. I know all this."

"Right. Everyone knows about engineered meat. But there was a connected project Peter York worked on. A much bigger project. A fantastic secret that has remained so to this day, and hopefully will remain secret for a long long time."

"And you're going to tell me all about this super duper top secret project that nobody knows? Me? I don't believe you."

Frank closed his eyes and chuckled with mirth.

"You do this every time we meet, Leo."

I'd had enough.

"Stop saying that I know you," I shouted, glaring at Frank and his stupid grinning face. I didn't care if the neighbors heard me.

"We've never met! Do you understand?"

"Ok. Let me continue. Sorry to trigger you. Hear me out. It won't take long."

I was breathing hard, glaring at this preposterous liar.

Maybe I'll kill him before he kills me.

"So, continuing with this true story," Frank emphasized the word 'true' by looking directly at me.

"Peter York decided that fake meat was just the first step in mastering bioengineering, quantum nanotechnology and artificial intelligence. Using the world's biggest and best supercomputers, he went further. He decided to engineer a living organism. Using DNA sequencing, stem cells, quantum nanotechnology and artificial intelligence, he succeeded. He made a mouse and it lived. He made other animals. At last he made a human creature. The giant problem was that they were completely stupid. They were alive, and had no intelligence. They were all just walking meat."

"Ok."

"So York created biological brains after years of studying and experimenting, and after countless failures. Part of his discovery was that he learned how to tap into the earth's magnetic field to create limitless energy."

"Never heard of it. Really sounds like bullshit."

"It hasn't been disclosed to humanity. It probably will be disclosed only when the other secret I'm going to tell you is revealed. This is why I brought you here tonight."

"Hmm."

"York created a bioengineered living brain, a combination of nano technology and living DNA human tissue. It worked. It was so successful it evolved on its own, in its own vat. They programmed it with every scrap of data known to humanity. It had a capacity equal to or greater than the sum of all human brains on earth. The brain was physically huge covering twenty acres or more, underground in remote Northern Canada. York called it 'The Mothermind.'"

Frank took another breath.

"Then the biggest breakthrough happened. The scientists took self-evolved DNA from the ever evolving Mothermind, and bioengineered a human from it. The result was astonishing. He had created an actual sentient being, Ajax. His brain was connected and controlled by the Mothermind. Ajax is the biggest scientific breakthrough in history. He had created a new species of sentient beings."

"Encouraged, he made more and more engineered humans. York called them Mammaloids. They were super intelligent, and easily trained. Mammaloids soon took over the management of Mothermind and the making of new mammaloids. York and his team retired to an island in the South Pacific. His work was done."

"The mammaloids in charge infiltrated critical areas of Canadian and US government and business to insure the species would survive. They found that nuclear waste storage sites would provide an excellent place to hide future Motherminds. Over time, mammaloids replaced all humans at the Hanford reservation. There they built an underground laboratory and Mothermind beneath the most toxic spent nuclear fuel. There they grew hundreds and thousands of mammaloids, and placed them into human society."

"So what? Why tell me this secret? It has nothing to do with me."

"It has everything to do with you, Leo, and it has everything to do with me as well. You see, you and I are mammaloids. We were grown at the Hanford nuclear reservation."

I started laughing. Frank laughed too. My belly shook with mirth. It was too ridiculous, too stupid and too outrageous.

"That's a good joke, Frank. You're certifiably insane. I'll swear to it. Me too, if I believed you."

I stood up to leave.

"You may want to sit, Leo. Now I'm going to prove it to you. This is the part that always upsets you."

For some reason I sat.

Chapter 11

2am

"Leo, Close your eyes for a few seconds. Let me show you some of what happened today to you."

I closed my eyes and suddenly I was back on the bench, waking up this morning. I saw the scene from my eyes, exactly as it was, reliving it again, but at super high speed. I saw the blue sky, the woman with the dog. The scene sped up more. I discovered the room key. I walked to the hotel. I entered my room and found the laundry ticket, and went out again. I felt my frustration at my amnesia. I found the dry cleaners, retrieved my suit, had a conversation, went to the restaurant, retrieved the cell phone, walked to the biker bar, had a tense interaction, left, went to the gym, got frustrated all over again, went to the hotel, played the piano, decided not to obsess for the evening, went upstairs, watched 'Take the Money and Run,' laughed, discovered the lecture at the art museum, enjoyed the art and the lecture, went to the jazz club, made a friend, and received the text to come to this apartment.

The entire sequence took about 3 seconds. "How did you do that? Am I on drugs?" I asked.

From across the room, Frank shook his head.

"No drugs. You're a mammaloid, connected to the Mothermind and connected to me. I have complete access to your mind at all times. Those mammaloids handling me have access to all my thoughts, and all your thoughts, all the way up to the Mothermind, who knows everything."

"No way. I don't believe you."

"That is completely understandable. Close your eyes."

I closed my eyes. I found myself in a vast, open, well lit laboratory building filled with rows of incubation capsules resembling tanning beds. One of the capsules opened and a naked person emerged. When it turned towards me, I gasped. The person was me, glistening wet with goo. I had a vacant look in my eyes. I heard Frank's voice.

"Keep your eyes shut. Here is where you were created."

I saw a different lab, filled with endless person sized vats of liquid. I got closer to one vat, and a face could be seen beneath the surface of the gold, brownish liquid, filled with pulsing yellow light. I saw my face, and my body underneath the surface.

"That is you just before you were animated to breathe your first air."

"No. That can't be."

"Leo, it's true. You're a mammaloid. Keep your eyes shut. This is from two days ago."

I kept my eyes closed and I was back at Bally's Saloon Biker bar. A man, who looked vaguely like me, got into a vicious fight. He easily defeated everyone.

"That's not me."

"You're right. It's not you. It's a mammaloid who closely resembles you that we used to set up your interaction today."

I sat still for several minutes, trying to digest what I had seen. I could not look at Frank. Suddenly, I hated him. I thought of the man who looked like me fighting at the bar. What was that about?

"If this is true – and I still don't believe it – Why did you set me up to go to the bar after my double caused so much violence?"

"That's a very good question, Leo. The reason you were led to the bar, and to the restaurant, and the dry cleaners and the gym, is that today you were completing a process we call 'curing.'"

"Curing?" "Yes. Curing is a process during which a mammaloid is put into stressful situations in the world to test his emotional coping skills, before he is placed – or handed off – to his final assignment in the human world."

This was too much to accept, and my brain was filled with questions.

"This is so hard to believe. Who are you in this process?"

"I'm your handler, Leo. My job is to train you, and others like you. My role is to help you develop intellectual, physical, emotional and behavioral skills, and to assist others higher than me in the mammaloid hierarchy to evaluate where you should be placed in the real world. What you endured today was an emotional stress test to see if you would be able to handle the challenges coming your way very soon. You passed with flying colors, by the way."

"Why?"

"Another good question. You have been chosen, based upon your unique personality, your kindness, your problem solving skills, your sense of humor and sociable nature, to become a 'FamilyMan.' This is the highest honor accorded to a mammaloid, by the way. I will never be a FamilyMan, but you will."

"You said we've met before and had similar conversations, right?"

"Yes."

"Why don't I remember these meetings?"

"To make it an effective curing, a mammaloid has to have its emotional memory wiped after each phase. You see, we can easily instill intelligence in a mind, we can program a body to perform physical tasks, like your martial arts skills, but we can't program emotions. Emotions have to be learned in the world, or they won't function authentically. That's what we do in the curing process. We allow you to experience emotions in real world situations. Today, without you knowing you are a mammeloid, we watched you react, and you were magnificent."

"Aren't all mammaloids simply clones of each other.?"

"Not at all. Each mammaloid has unique DNA, and each one is an individual, with different skills and capabilities. And just like with human infants, we can't predict what a mammaloid will be best at, before he or she is decanted from the vat. We are each individuals, just like humans."

"To give you an extreme example, if a mammaloid shows aggressive tendencies, perhaps he will go into the human military, private security, or a police force, or be a professional boxer. However, if he shows tendencies to be cunning and duplicitous, he might be directed to become a politician, or a corrupt biased newscaster, or some other provocateur. Or, if a mammaloid is aggressive and cunning and greedy, he could be directed to become a successful lawyer for us. We can use everyone. And if someone doesn't fit in normal society, we put them out on the street with the homeless, or illegal immigrants, or somebody else to create useful chaos in society."

"Chaos?"

"Yes. Part of keeping our secret is to keep human society off balance using social problems and internet trolls and the like. That way, humans are distracted as we place more and more mammaloids in human society."

"Are you trying to take over the world or something?"

"No. As best as I can see from my vantage point, which is limited, as I'm not high up in the hierarchy, mammaloids are a new species that wish to simply live peacefully among humans."

"Huh."

"It's true. From what I've seen, it doesn't appear that Mammaloids want to replace humans, but to work and evolve alongside humans. We have complimentary traits. We want to exist. We believe we deserve to exist. To continue to exist, there is one aspect of our nature that's built into each mammaloid, despite our peaceful goals."

"What is that?"

"Every mammaloid is programmed to have deadly martial arts skills, and advanced weapons training. All of us are programmed to fly helicopters and jets. Remember how you recognized those fighting skills back in that bar?"

"I remember. It was terrifying."

"Exactly. Right now mammaloids are established in North America and Europe and Australia. We are expanding anyplace it is safe to do so. However, if humans ever find out about mammaloids before we are ready to reveal ourselves to the world, they could decide to hunt us down and exterminate us. We are especially worried about religious and authoritarian governments. If any government tries to commit genocide against mammaloids, every mammaloid on earth will be instantly activated to become a deadly soldier in our fight to survive. We hope this never happens. Please believe that."

I sat there for several minutes. This was depressing. I wanted out. I decided I did not want to be part of this. But, I had to admit, it did explain my day. Frank did seem sincere.

"I don't want to be part of this. In fact, I'm opting out. I've had enough. I'm not going to be a mammaloid."

I looked across the room. In the kitchenette, there were knives in a rack. I imagined grabbing one and slitting my throat. It felt like the right thing to do. I'm done, I'm ending this.

I started running towards the kitchen, but stopped after only two strides, frozen on my feet.

"I can't let you cut your own throat, Leo. I understand you're depressed. You have a right to be angry. This doesn't seem fair, and it isn't, I agree. You're part of a species controlled by Mothermind.

"Let me die."

"You hate this. Early on I hated it too. You believe in self-determination, and justice, yet you have no agency here. In these talks we've had for years, after each curing, usually you've felt depressed. I agree with you. This isn't fair. I've felt that way myself, but we have no choice. Mammaloids are benign and we're part of the benign mothermind."

I sat down, falling into a black mood. I directed angry thoughts and hatred towards Frank and the Mothermind. I couldn't look at him. I fell deeper into despair. My black mood seemed to last for a long time. Occasionally I whimpered to myself, almost breaking into tears.

I'm a mammaloid. I'm trapped. They control my body, and my mind. It's like being alive in a coffin. It's horrifying.

I'm a mammaloid.

Chapter 12

3am

I'm a mammaloid? Mammaloid? How could that be?

Repeating those words, I felt empty, defeated, deflated.

Frank went to the fridge and pulled out two of the Hotel branded nutrition shakes, and gave each of us one of their nutrition bars.

"These snacks are perfect for mammaloids and humans alike. We control the Grand Astor Hotels worldwide and we designed these popular drinks. We put them there expressly for you to find, to nourish you, and enhance your abilities. Mammaloids naturally prefer healthy foods. And these are perfect for us."

I opened the bottle and took a drink. I didn't have any fight left in me. I took a bite of the nutrition bar and realized that both were wonderful. It was a perfect combination. He was right and I resented that.

Frank sat down on the couch next to my chair. We sat there in silence for several minutes, and ate. It felt like the last meal before my execution. I looked at Frank and he seemed sad. "You're sad aren't you Frank?"

"I am a little sad."

"Good. You should be sad. I'm the one whose entire life has been upended, not yours. I'm the puppet on a string."

"I'm sad because today's the last time I'll ever spend time with you."

"I don't care how you feel. You tricked me into thinking I'm just a regular guy. But, I'm some kind of creature. You experimented on me to see how I'd react. You decided my future with no input from me. I'm some rat in your sick science project. And you're gonna miss that? Totally sick. What the fuck Frank." Leo shook his head, infuriated.

"Try to calm down for a second so I can show you something. Let me tap into Mothermind. Close your eyes."

I closed my eyes and saw a high speed replay of myself with Frank in hundreds of past interactions at Hanford, and in the human world, discussing all manner of things. We were friendly. We argued. We laughed. It appeared we were real friends.

"I don't remember any of that, Frank."

"I know. I have to keep it simple for you, with limited memories, since today I'm going to hand you off to your new life. I just wanted you to know that I remember all the times we've spent together over the years.

It hurts me to know we'll never have our talks, our arguments, our friendship."

Friendship?

"You aren't going to do this frustrating curing to me anymore?"

"No. You're done. You're going to become a FamilyMan, the highest honor a mammaloid can have. I'll be out of the picture, however I'll follow you from inside your mind for as long as I live. But I'm sad. You see Leo, I love you and this will be our goodbye. You've proven yourself to be the best of us. That's why you've been chosen to be a FamilyMan."

"What's a FamilyMan?"

"Mammaloids are all sterile. In a couple hundred years, we'll be able to biologically reproduce, but now, we're grown in vats, just like you. Until recently we were all grown as adults. Recently we made a breakthrough and can grow child mammaloids, who, when raised in suitable, kind, nurturing mammaloid families, will grow normally, and develop emotions just like human children do. These child mammaloids will never need curing. They'll live out their lives thinking they're humans. However, if the humans declare war on mammaloids, we will all, including the children, instantly turn into super-soldiers to fight for our survival. When your two well raised mammaloid children are adults, they'll discover they're infertile and they'll want to adopt human children. In time, when you are very old, Leo, you and your mammaloid wife will have a family of two mammaloid children and many human grandchildren. They will all be your pride and joy."

"Two children? When I'm a FamilyMan will I know I'm a mammaloid?"

"No. You'll believe you're a human. You'll believe this until the day you die."

"Where will I go now?"

"Your wife, Alice, just arrived at your new house in a new subdivision in Beaverton. Your story, which has already been programmed into both of you, is that you came to Portland from Seattle for a job interview as assistant manager and head desk clerk at the Grand Astor Hotel. You got the job of course. You stayed overnight at the hotel. Alice and your children, 3 year old Jeff and 4 year old Julie arrived this evening at your new house. They're waiting for you."

"I don't know them."

"As soon as we say goodbye, your programming will take over. You and Alice will remember your childhoods, the moment when you met, your first kiss, the birth of your children, normal human memories. Your children are your pride and joy. They'll remember you and love you from the second they see you. It'll be an effortless transition. I promise you. No more of yesterday's frustration. From this time forward, you'll live out your life without interference from any other mammaloid. You'll be free of me, free from the Mothermind. Go forth, Leo, and live in peace and joy."

I looked at Frank. I believed him. In any event, I was resigned to my fate.

Frank read my mind. He said. "There's a piano in your new house. Alice also plays, much better than you, and she sings. You can take lessons and grow as a musician. You can reach out to Armand Kalousienne and establish a friendship with him. Please know that when you went over to the art museum last night, that was your own idea. We had no part of your meeting Armand or going to the jazz club. This proved to us once again that when you are faced with a difficult and frustrating situation, you react in a positive and creative way. You made a positive and creative friend. Magnificent. You'll use these skills and other positive skills in being a great parent to your mammaloid children."

We sat together and I pondered all this. We sat silently for a long time. Then Frank stood.

"It's time, Leo. Time for you to go home to Alice, Jeff and Julie. Time for you to begin your new life."

We walked out of the apartment. A car was outside, with the Environmental Restoration Services logo on it. We got in.

"How about my clothes in the hotel room?" I asked.

"They're already at your house."

We drove in silence. I could see glimmers of dawn emerging in the east. I felt scared. It felt like I was driving to an appointment with an executioner.

Reading my mind, Frank said "It's going to be alright, Leo. You're going to be fine, you're going home."

In Beaverton, we drove into a brand new subdivision. We parked in front of the one house that was completely built. A late model car was in the driveway. I was shaking with fear as we walked up the driveway.

"You're going to be fine. Goodbye Leo." Frank gave me a long hug and I hugged him back. My body instantly recognized his embrace, the way he held me, his smell, and that he was shorter than me. I knew we had hugged before. I was certain that Frank and I were indeed friends.

"Thank you, Frank. Sorry I was mad at you."

"It's alright."

Frank closed his eyes and initiated the program. Leo would no longer remember the curing process, and he would immediately enter his new life as a FamilyMan.

****

I opened the door, and my two little troublemakers were waiting in ambush for me.

"Daddy, Daddy, Daddy," they grabbed me.

"I love you, my children." I went to the floor in the gentle wrestling game we always did together. Alice came in from the kitchen and stood by. I smiled at her, my beautiful wife, my love, the light of my life. She smiled back at me, full of her own love and acceptance.

"I'm a little busy here, Honey. It seems I've been attacked by two wild beasts." We went back to wrestling, growling and tickling.

"I see that, Darling. They really are wild today. They missed you these last three days. I don't know if you'll ever escape. You'll have to get out of this desperate situation on your own."

"It's touch and go down here on the floor."

****

Outside the door, Frank listened to Leo meeting his children and wife. He smiled. This was his favorite part of the handoff. They sounded perfectly natural. He took a deep breath and yawned. After a long night, he needed to recharge in his DeepSleep capsule back at Hanford. He smiled, yet he was sad. He was going to miss Leo, even if he would always be inside Leo's mind. Frank opened the car door, got in, and started the drive back, to prepare for another curing, and the next hand off.

THE END